FORGET-ME-NOTS

Poems to Learn by Heart

Selected by Mary Ann Hoberman

Illustrated by Michael Emberley

Megan Tingley Books
LITTLE, BROWN AND COMPANY
New York   Boston

TABLE OF CONTENTS

Introduction

DELICIOUS DISHES

IT'S ABOUT TIME

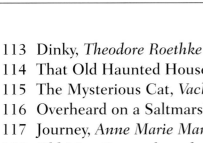

POEMS FROM STORYBOOKS

THE LONG OF IT

**Some Suggestions for
Learning Poetry by Heart**

Index of First Lines

Acknowledgments

INTRODUCTION

When you learn a poem by heart, it becomes a part of you. You know it in your mind, in your mouth, in your ears, in your whole body. And best of all, you know it forever.

When you memorize a poem, it is almost as if you have entered the poet's mind. As you say the poem over and over, you begin to understand why the poet chose one word and not another. You notice how certain sounds repeat themselves and knit the lines together. It's a little like figuring out a puzzle, and, like a good puzzle, it's fun!

With your eyes freed from the page, you can really feel the poem's rhythm. It is probably no accident that we talk of learning poems "by heart." Like our hearts, most poems have a steady beat. Sometimes it helps to clap your hands to the poem's rhythm as you recite it.

The poems in this book are for both the beginning reader and the more experienced reader. Some are short, others long; some are simple, others a bit more complicated. Some are funny, others serious. But all of them were chosen because they are *memorable*.

Memorable has two meanings: "easy to remember" and "worth remembering." While some poems will take longer to memorize than others, all of them have been chosen with ease of memorization in mind. And more important, all of them are worth remembering. Whether they are exciting or peaceful, puzzling or just plain silly, you will find they catch your interest—probably not every single one of them, but enough to give you a wide choice.

You might begin with some of the short poems you'll find throughout the book. After you have learned a few of these, you can go on to some longer ones. Long poems are not necessarily harder to memorize. They often tell a story, are strongly rhythmical, and have a lot of repetition, all helpful for learning by heart.

At the end of the book, I talk about different methods of memorization. You might want to refer to that when you are ready to go on to some of the more complex poems.

START

YOU'RE

FOR TH

8

A POEM FOR T

SILLY ONE

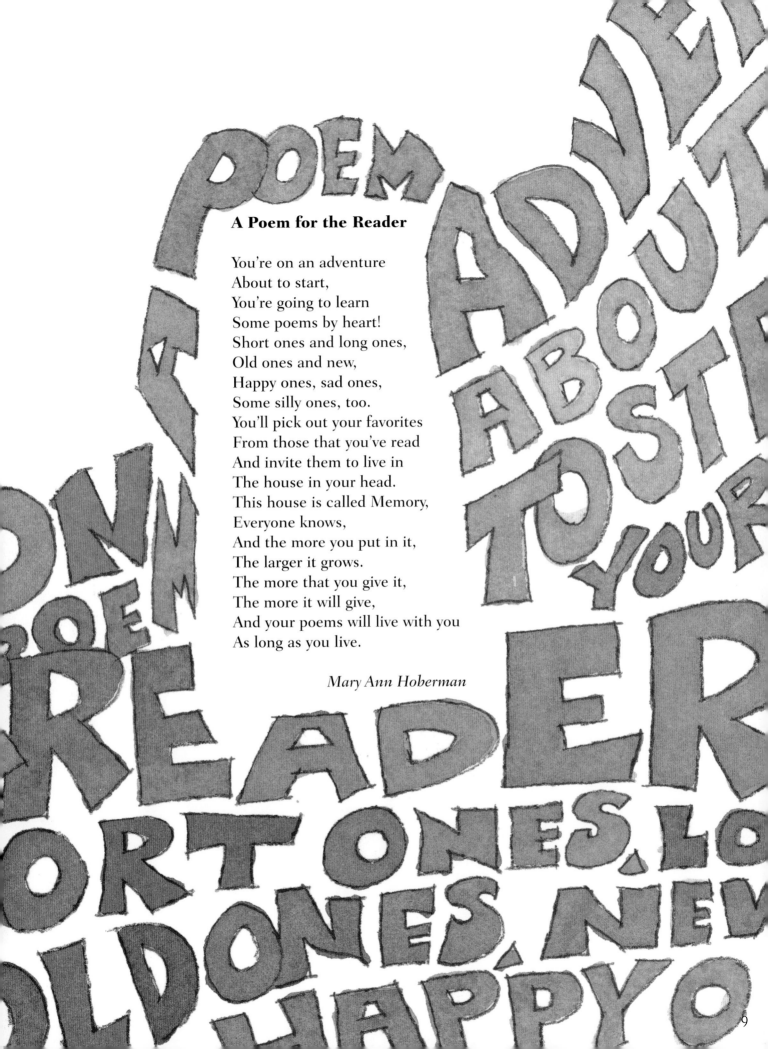

A Poem for the Reader

You're on an adventure
About to start,
You're going to learn
Some poems by heart!
Short ones and long ones,
Old ones and new,
Happy ones, sad ones,
Some silly ones, too.
You'll pick out your favorites
From those that you've read
And invite them to live in
The house in your head.
This house is called Memory,
Everyone knows,
And the more you put in it,
The larger it grows.
The more that you give it,
The more it will give,
And your poems will live with you
As long as you live.

Mary Ann Hoberman

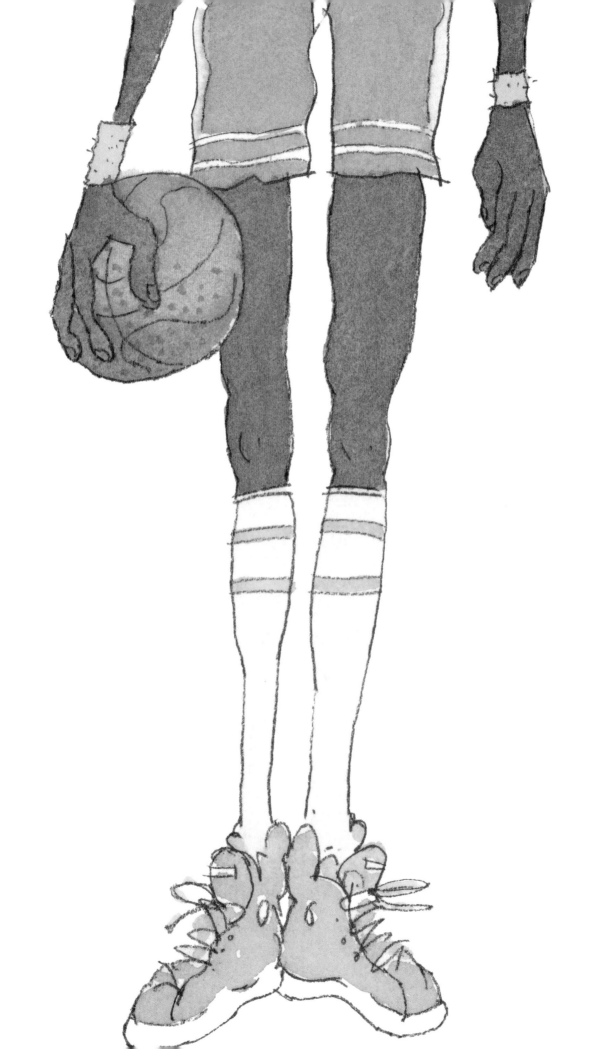

THE SHORT OF IT

These first poems are very short, so they are quite easy to memorize. Just say them a few times to yourself and before you know it, you'll have them by heart!

Auk Talk

The raucous auk must squawk to talk.
The squawk auks squawk to talk goes
AUK!

      Mary Ann Hoberman

Rain

The rain is raining all around,
    It falls on field and tree,
It rains on the umbrellas here,
    And on the ships at sea.

      Robert Louis Stevenson

A word is dead

A word is dead
When it is said,
Some say.
I say it just
Begins to live
That day.

Emily Dickinson

Primer Lesson

Look out how you use proud words.
When you let proud words go, it is not easy to call them back.
They wear long boots, hard boots; they walk off proud; they
    can't hear you calling—
Look out how you use proud words.

Carl Sandburg

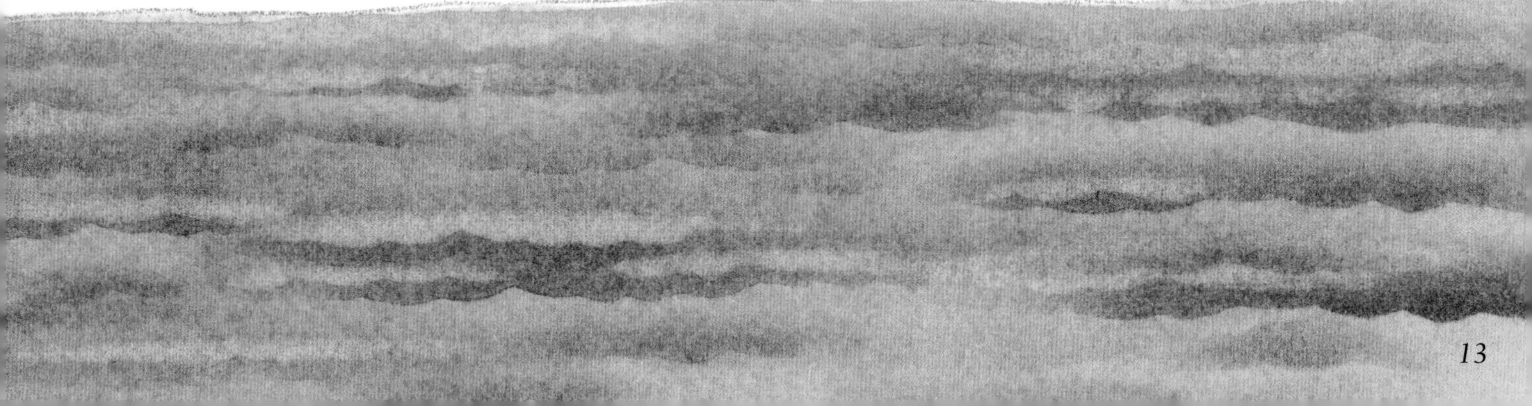

If all the world were paper

If all the world were paper
And all the sea were ink
And all the trees were bread and cheese,
What should we have to drink?

Anonymous

There was an old person of Ware

There was an old person of Ware,
Who rode on the back of a bear:
When they asked, "Does it trot?"
He said, "Certainly not!
He's a Moppsikon Floppsikon bear!"

Edward Lear

To His Cat

With huggings, and a last "Achoo!"
My dearest cat, I part from you.
I love your paws, I love your purr,
But I'm allergic to your fur.

Doris Orgel

Hippopotamus

How far from human beauty
Is the hairless hippopotamus
With such a square enormous head
And such a heavy botamus.

Mary Ann Hoberman

The Little Man Who Wasn't There

Last night I saw upon the stair
A little man who wasn't there
He wasn't there again today
Oh, how I wish he'd go away

Hughes Mearns

The Floorless Room

I wish that my room had a floor;
I don't so much care for a door,
But this walking around
Without touching the ground
Is getting to be quite a bore!

Gelett Burgess

There was an old man of Blackheath

There was an old man of Blackheath,
Who sat on his set of false teeth.
    Said he, with a start,
    "O Lord, bless my heart!
I've bitten myself underneath!"

Anonymous

Fireflies

Fireflies at twilight
In search of one another
Twinkle off and on.

Mary Ann Hoberman

ONE AND ALL

Here are some poems about people—children and grown-ups, family and friends. In some of them you may find feelings and thoughts you have had yourself. Others give you insights into other people's experiences and ideas. Some are serious and some are silly—and some are both at the same time!

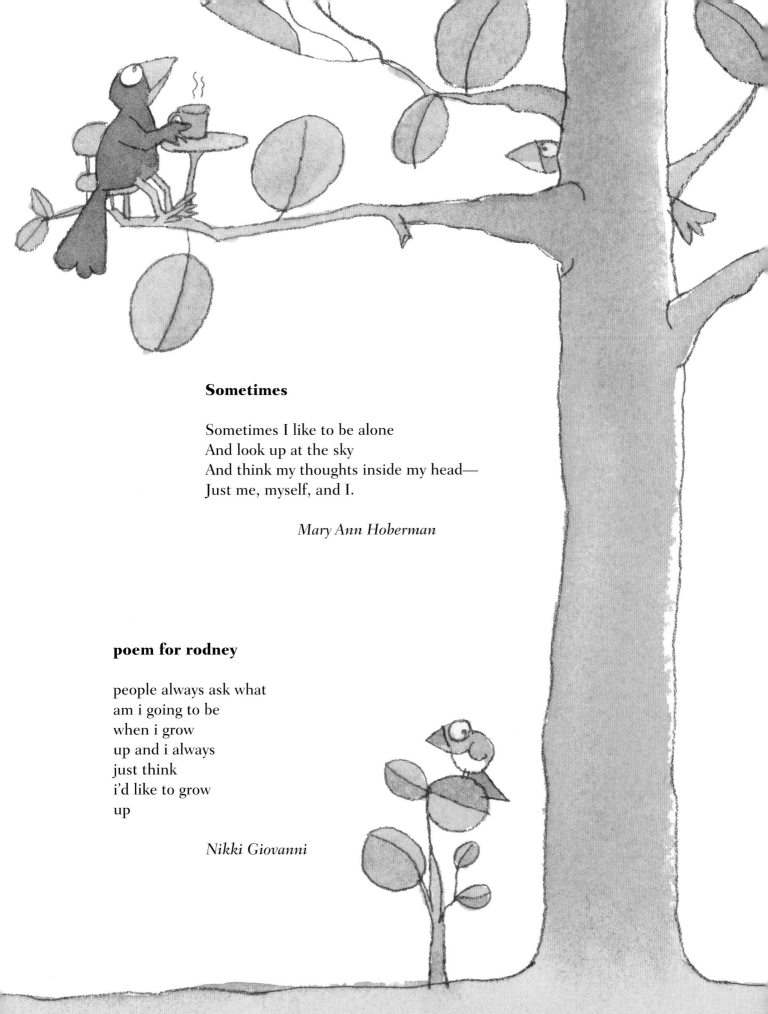

Sometimes

Sometimes I like to be alone
And look up at the sky
And think my thoughts inside my head—
Just me, myself, and I.

Mary Ann Hoberman

poem for rodney

people always ask what
am i going to be
when i grow
up and i always
just think
i'd like to grow
up

Nikki Giovanni

San Francisco

yo me llamo
Francisco
como mi abuelo

y como
el abuelo
de su abuelo

cómo me alegro
que esta ciudad
lleve el nombre

de San Francisco—
el santo patrón
de los animales

aquí mi nombre
todos lo saben
escribir

San Francisco

my name is
Francisco like
my grandfather

and like
his grandfather's
grandfather

I'm so happy
this city is
named after

Saint Francis—
the patron saint
of all animals

here everybody
knows how to
spell my name

Francisco X. Alarcón

My Name

I wrote my name on the sidewalk
But the rain washed it away.

I wrote my name on my hand
But the soap washed it away.

I wrote my name on the birthday card
I gave to Mother today

And there it will stay
For mother never throws

ANYTHING

of mine away!

Lee Bennett Hopkins

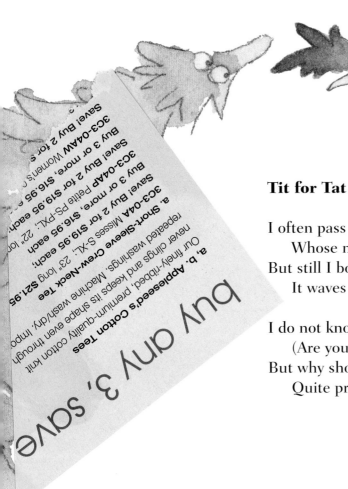

Tit for Tat

I often pass a gracious tree
    Whose name I can't identify,
But still I bow, in courtesy
    It waves a bough, in kind reply.

I do not know your name, O tree
    (Are you a hemlock or a pine?)
But why should that embarrass me?
    Quite probably you don't know mine.

        Christopher Morley

Strategy

I went to class, sat in a chair
That wobbled and rocked. Got up

And changed seats.
I got up again, and again.

That's how I happened
To sit next to you.

    Gary Soto

You Oughta Meet Danitra Brown

You oughta meet Danitra Brown,
the most splendiferous girl in town.
I oughta know, 'cause she's my friend.

She's not afraid to take a dare.
If something's hard, she doesn't care.
She'll try her best, no matter what.

She doesn't mind what people say.
She always does things her own way.
Her spirit's old, my mom once said.

I only know I like her best
'cause she sticks out from all the rest.
She's only she—Danitra Brown.

Nikki Grimes

A Time to Talk

When a friend calls to me from the road
And slows his horse to a meaning walk,
I don't stand still and look around
On all the hills I haven't hoed,
And shout from where I am, "What is it?"
No, not as there is a time to talk.
I thrust my hoe in the mellow ground,
Blade-end up and five feet tall,
And plod: I go up to the stone wall
For a friendly visit.

Robert Frost

The Twins

The two-ones is the name for it,
And that is what it ought to be,
But when you say it very fast
It makes your lips say twins you see.

When I was just a little thing,
About the year before the last,
I called it two-ones all the time,
But now I always say it fast.

Elizabeth Madox Roberts

Love That Boy

Love that boy,
like a rabbit loves to run
I said I love that boy
like a rabbit loves to run
Love to call him in the morning
love to call him
"Hey there, son!"

He walk like his grandpa
grins like his uncle Ben
I said he walk like his grandpa
and grins like his uncle Ben
Grins when he happy
when he sad he grins again

His mama like to hold him
like to feed him cherry pie
I said his mama like to hold him
feed him that cherry pie
She can have him now
I'll get him by and by

He got long roads to walk down,
before the setting sun
I said he got a long, long road to walk down,
before the setting sun
He'll be a long stride walker
and a good man before he done

Walter Dean Myers

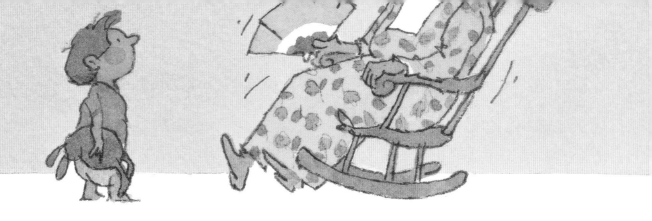

Antique Shop

I knew an old lady
A long time ago
Who rocked while she told me
The things I should know.

She lies in her grave now
And I am a man
But here is her rocker
And here is her fan.

Her fan and her rocker
Are all that remain
But I can still see her
Rock-rocking,
Talk-talking,
Rock-rocking
Again.

Carl Carmer

Nancy Hanks

If Nancy Hanks
Came back as a ghost,
Seeking news
Of what she loved most,
She'd ask first
"Where's my son?
What's happened to Abe?
What's he done?

"Poor little Abe,
Left all alone
Except for Tom,
Who's a rolling stone;
He was only nine
The year I died.
I remember still
How hard he cried.

"Scraping along
In a little shack,
With hardly a shirt
To cover his back,
And a prairie wind
To blow him down,
Or pinching times
If he went to town.

"You wouldn't know
About my son?
Did he grow tall?
Did he have fun?
Did he learn to read?
Did he get to town?
Do you know his name?
Did he get on?"

*Rosemary and
Stephen Vincent Benét*

I'm nobody! Who are you?

I'm nobody! Who are you?
Are you nobody, too?
Then there's a pair of us—don't tell!
They'd banish us, you know.

How dreary to be somebody!
How public, like a frog
To tell your name the livelong day
To an admiring bog!

Emily Dickinson

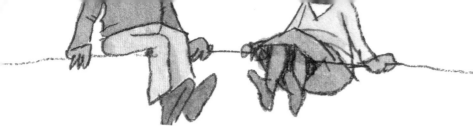

Bird Talk

"Think…" said the robin,
"Think…" said the jay,
sitting in the garden,
talking one day.

"Think about people—
the way they grow:
they don't have feathers
at all, you know.

"They don't eat beetles,
they don't grow wings,
they don't like sitting
on wires and things.

"Think!" said the robin.
"Think!" said the jay.
"Aren't people funny
to be that way?"

Aileen Fisher

Messages from Everywhere

light up our backyard.
A bird that flew five thousand miles
is trilling six bright notes.
This bird flew over mountains and valleys
and tiny dolls and pencils
of children I will never see.
Because this bird is singing to me,
I belong to the wide wind,
the people far away who share
the air and the clouds.
Together we are looking up
into all we do not own
and we are listening.

Naomi Shihab Nye

BEAUTIFUL BEASTS

Is there a poet anywhere who hasn't written about animals? Thousands of years ago, Aesop was writing his short animal fables; and animals both domestic and wild have always been one of poetry's favorite subjects. And as you will see here, they have inspired some wonderful poems for memorizing.

The Animal Store

If I had a hundred dollars to spend,
    Or maybe a little more,
I'd hurry as fast as my legs would go
    Straight to the animal store.

I wouldn't say, "How much for this or that?"—
    "What kind of a dog is he?"
I'd buy as many as rolled an eye,
    Or wagged a tail at me!

I'd take the hound with the drooping ears
    That sits by himself alone;
Cockers and Cairns and wobbly pups
    For to be my very own.

I might buy a parrot all red and green,
    And the monkey I saw before,
If I had a hundred dollars to spend,
    Or maybe a little more.

Rachel Field

Chums

He sits and begs; he gives a paw;
　　He is, as you can see,
The finest dog you ever saw,
　　And he belongs to me.

He follows everywhere I go
　　And even when I swim.
I laugh because he thinks, you know,
　　That I belong to him.

But still, no matter what we do,
　　We never have a fuss,
And so I guess it must be true
　　That *we* belong to *us*.

Arthur Guiterman

My Cat

My cat is asleep—white paws
folded under
his chin   He is a soft gray
smudge on the round rug

Dozing in the sun
He is a warm round stone
with a fur collar

My cat is taking
a nap   Not a whisker
trembles   Not a hair
moves   His breath goes
softly in and out

Stay in your holes
mice!   My cat sees you
in his dreams
and he has left
his motor running!

Barbara Esbensen

Roosters

"Get out of my way!"
    says Rooster One.
"I won't!"
    says Rooster Two.
"You won't?"
"I won't!"
"You shall!"
"I shan't!"
Cock cock a
doodle doo!

They pecked.
They kicked.
They fought for hours.
There was a great
to-do!
"You're a very fine fighter,"
    says Rooster One.
"You're right!"
    says Rooster Two.

Elizabeth Coatsworth

Mary Middling

Mary Middling had a pig,
Not very little and not very big,
Not very pink, not very green,
Not very dirty, not very clean,
Not very good, not very naughty,
Not very humble, not very haughty,
Not very thin, not very fat;
Now what would you give for a pig like that?

Rose Fyleman

A Frog in a Well
Explains the World

The world is round
and deep
and cool.
The bottom of the world's
a pool
with just enough room
for a frog alone.
The walls of the world
are of stone on stone.
At the top of the world,
when I look up high,
I can see a star
in a little round sky.

Alice Schertle

Bat Patrol

Quickly and quietly,
the bat patrols the night,
sending an invisible song
echoing like ripples on a pond,
chasing moths around a streetlight.
Quickly and quietly,
the bat patrols the night.

Georgia Heard

The Little Turtle

There was a little turtle.
He lived in a box.
He swam in a puddle.
He climbed on the rocks.

He snapped at a mosquito.
He snapped at a flea.
He snapped at a minnow.
And he snapped at me.

He caught the mosquito.
He caught the flea.
He caught the minnow.
But he didn't catch me.

Vachel Lindsay

Beavers in November

This stick   here
That stick   there
    Mud, more mud, add mud, good mud
That stick   here
This stick   there
    Mud, more mud, add mud, good mud
        You pat
        I gnaw
        I pile
        You store
This stick   here
That stick   there
    Mud, more mud, add mud, good mud
        You guard
        I pack
        I dig
        You stack
That stick   here
This stick   there
    Mud, more mud, add mud, good mud
        I trim
        You mold
        To keep
        Out cold
This stick   here
That stick   there
    Mud, more mud, add mud, good mud

Marilyn Singer

41

The Puffin

A puffin loves stuffin'
Its bill full of fishes.
It fills it with seven
Or eight if it wishes.
It always finds dishes
Of fishes delicious.
A puffin loves stuffin'
Its bill full of fishes.

Douglas Florian

Don't Ever Seize a Weasel by the Tail

You should never squeeze a weasel
for you might displease the weasel,
and don't ever seize a weasel by the tail.

Let his tail blow in the breeze;
if you pull it, he will sneeze,
for the weasel's constitution tends to be a little frail.

Yes the weasel wheezes easily;
the weasel freezes easily;
the weasel's tan complexion rather suddenly turns pale.

So don't displease or tease a weasel,
squeeze or freeze or wheeze a weasel
and don't ever seize a weasel by the tail.

Jack Prelutsky

Tiger

I'm a tiger
Striped with fur
Don't come near
Or I might *Grrr*
Don't come near
Or I might growl
Don't come near
Or I might
BITE!

Mary Ann Hoberman

The Yak

As a friend to the children commend me the Yak.
   You will find it exactly the thing:
It will carry and fetch, you can ride on its back,
   Or lead it about with a string.

The Tartar who dwells on the plains of Thibet
   (A desolate region of snow)
Has for centuries made it a nursery pet,
   And surely the Tartar should know!

Then tell your papa where the Yak can be got,
   And if he is awfully rich
He will buy you the creature—or else he will *not*.
   (I cannot be positive which.)

Hilaire Belloc

Eletelephony

Once there was an elephant,
Who tried to use the telephant—
No! no! I mean an elephone
Who tried to use the telephone—
(Dear me! I am not certain quite
That even now I've got it right.)

Howe'er it was, he got his trunk
Entangled in the telephunk;
The more he tried to get it free,
The louder buzzed the telephee—
(I fear I'd better drop the song
Of elephop and telephong!)

Laura E. Richards

DELICIOUS DISHES

Poems about food are usually funny (ha ha). That's
a little funny (odd) in itself, since getting enough to
eat has always been a very serious matter for most of
the people in the world. But somehow when poets
write about food, they generally look at the lighter side
of things. However, keep your eyes open! Tucked in
among the comical poems are a few that approach the
subject quite differently.

I eat my peas with honey

I eat my peas with honey
I've done it all my life.
It makes the peas taste funny
But it keeps them on the knife.

Anonymous

Oak Leaf Plate

Oak leaf plate
Acorn cup
Raindrop tea
Drink it up!

Sand for salt
Mud for pie
Twiggy chops
Fine to fry.

Sticks for bread
Stones for meat
Grass for greens
Time to eat!

Mary Ann Hoberman

Mix a Pancake

Mix a pancake,
Stir a pancake,
    Pop it in the pan;
Fry the pancake,
Toss the pancake—
    Catch it if you can.

Christina Rossetti

Yellow Butter

Yellow butter purple jelly red jam black bread

Spread it thick
Say it quick

Yellow butter purple jelly red jam black bread

Spread it thicker
Say it quicker

Yellow butter purple jelly red jam black bread

Now repeat it
While you eat it

Yellow butter purple jelly red jam black bread

Don't talk
With your mouth full!

Mary Ann Hoberman

The Silver Fish

While fishing in the blue lagoon
I caught a lovely silver fish,
And he spoke to me. "My boy," quoth he,
"Please set me free and I'll grant your wish…
A kingdom of wisdom? A palace of gold?
Or all the goodies your fancies can hold?"
So I said, "OK," and I threw him free,
And he swam away and he laughed at me
Whispering my foolish wish
Into a silent sea.
Today I caught that fish again,
That lovely silver prince of fishes,
And once again he offered me—
If I would only set him free—
Any one of a number of wonderful wishes….
He was delicious!

Shel Silverstein

Alas, Alack!

Ann, Ann!
    Come quick as you can!
There's a fish that *talks*
    In the frying pan.
Out of the fat,
    As clear as glass,
He put up his mouth
    And moaned "Alas!"
Oh, most mournful,
    "Alas, alack!"
Then turned to his sizzling
    And sank him back.

Walter de la Mare

Raw Carrots

Raw carrots taste
Cool and hard,
Like some crisp metal.

Horses are
Fond of them,
Crunching up

The red gold
With much wet
Juice and noise.

Carrots must taste
To horses
As they do to us.

Valerie Worth

Soup

I saw a famous man eating soup.
I say he was lifting a fat broth
Into his mouth with a spoon.
His name was in the newspapers that day
Spelled out in tall black headlines
And thousands of people were talking about him.

    When I saw him,
He sat bending his head over a plate
Putting soup in his mouth with a spoon.

Carl Sandburg

My Father Owns the Butcher Shop

My father owns the butcher shop,
My mother cuts the meat,
And I'm the little hot dog
That runs around the street.

Anonymous

Miss T.

It's a very odd thing—
    It's as odd as can be—
That whatever Miss T. eats
    Turns into Miss T.;
Porridge and apples,
    Mince, muffins and mutton,
Jam, junket, jumbles—
    Not a rap, not a button
It matters; the moment
    They're out of her plate,
Though shared by Miss Butcher
    And sour Mr. Bate;
Tiny and cheerful,
    And neat as can be,
Whatever Miss T. eats
    Turns into Miss T.

Walter de la Mare

Old Quin Queeribus

Old Quin Queeribus—
    He loved his garden so,
He wouldn't have a rake around,
    A shovel or a hoe.

For each potato's eyes he bought
    Fine spectacles of gold,
And mufflers for the corn, to keep
    Its ears from getting cold.

On every head of lettuce green—
    What do you think of that?—
And every head of cabbage, too,
    He tied a garden hat.

Old Quin Queeribus—
    He loved his garden so,
He couldn't eat his growing things,
    He only let them grow!

Nancy Byrd Turner

Found and Lost

I found a big red apple.
I took a great big bite.
But when I saw what I had bit,
I lost my appetite!

Anne Marie Manfried

To a Poor Old Woman

munching a plum on
the street a paper bag
of them in her hand

They taste good to her
They taste good
to her. They taste
good to her

You can see it by
the way she gives herself
to the one half
sucked out in her hand

Comforted
a solace of ripe plums
seeming to fill the air
They taste good to her

William Carlos Williams

Pretty Futility

Pretty Futility
Always declares

There's nothing so good
As a basket of pears,

Nothing so tranquil
Nothing so sweet

As eating ripe pears
In the quiet of heat.

She straightens her ruffles
She smiles as she swings,

And when she has eaten
Futility sings.

Elizabeth Coatsworth

CORK 15:50

BELFAST 13:40

GALWAY 20:20

GREYSTONES 1:10

DINGLE 21:30

BELFAST 20:01

13:50

SYDNEY 9:12   BOSTON 11:00

PARIS 11:21   BERLIN 13:30

←DEPARTURES←   →ARRIVALS→

IT'S ABOUT TIME

Time is such a puzzle. An hour can feel like a minute, and a minute can feel like an hour, depending on what you're doing and how you feel. And it's constantly changing—day turns into night, spring into summer, fall into winter. And as it changes, you're changing, too!

Time

Listen to the clock strike
One
    two
        three,
Up in the tall tower
One
    two
        three.
Hear the hours slowly chime;
Watch the hands descend and climb;
Listen to the sound of time
One
    two
        three.

Mary Ann Hoberman

Marie Lucille

That clock is ticking
Me away!
The me that only
Yesterday
Ate peanuts, jam and
Licorice
Is gone already.
And this is
'Cause nothing's putting
Back, each day,
The me that clock is
Ticking away.

Gwendolyn Brooks

The Early Morning

The moon on the one hand, the dawn on the other:
The moon is my sister, the dawn is my brother.
The moon on my left and the dawn on my right—
My brother, good morning; my sister, good night.

Hilaire Belloc

Time to Rise

A birdie with a yellow bill
    Hopped upon the windowsill,
Cocked his shining eye and said:
    "Ain't you 'shamed, you sleepy-head!"

Robert Louis Stevenson

Hurry

Hurry! says the morning,
don't be late for school!

Hurry! says the teacher,
hand in papers now!

Hurry! says the mother,
supper's getting cold!

Hurry! says the father,
time to go to bed!

Slowly, says the darkness,
you can talk to me...

Eve Merriam

The Days Have Names

The days have names,
the months have names,
and so do clouds and hurricanes.

But not the weeks:
of weekly names
nobody speaks—

it doesn't seem to bother us
that weeks pass by,
anonymous.

JonArno Lawson

Night

Stars over snow,
    And in the west a planet
Swinging below a star—
    Look for a lovely thing and you will find it,
It is not far—
    It never will be far.

        Sara Teasdale

The Oak Trees Are Dreaming

It is night
The oak trees are dreaming

In their deep night dream-sleep they mumble

They mumble a windsong of fireflies
They mumble a dreamsong of fireflies

They mumble a windsong of moonfire
They mumble a dreamsong of starfire

The leaves dream: dark dreams thick dreams
The trunks dream: light dreams fluttering dreams
The limbs dream: deep dreams tangled dreams
The roots dream: sky dreams   sun dreams

It is night
The oak trees are dreaming

Patricia Hubbell

At Night

At night,
when a branch scratches
against the screen,

I lie in bed listening
as my tree whispers:

*Night is happening
outside your window.*

Kristine O'Connell George

Sweet Dreams

I wonder as into bed I creep
What it feels like to fall asleep.
I've told myself stories, I've counted sheep,
But I'm always asleep when I fall asleep.
Tonight my eyes I will open keep,
And I'll stay awake till I fall asleep,
Then I'll know what it feels like to fall asleep,
Asleep,
Asleeep,
Asleeeep…

Ogden Nash

Magic Story for Falling Asleep

When the last giant came out of his cave
and his bones turned into the mountain
and his clothes turned into the flowers,

nothing was left but his tooth
which my dad took home in his truck
which my granddad carved into a bed

which my mom tucks me into at night
when I dream of the last giant
when I fall asleep on the mountain.

Nancy Willard

How Far

How far
How far
How far is today
When tomorrow has come
And it's yesterday?

Far
And far
And far away.

Mary Ann Hoberman

HAPPINESS IS

The poems in this section all have to do in some
way with joy. If you're already happy, they'll make
you happier. If you're feeling sad, they'll remind
you of the many different kinds of happiness there
are, from having a perfect outfit to wear on a rainy
day to walking up a beautiful hill in the sunshine to
lying on the kitchen floor, making up a poem. And
best of all, the feeling of loving and being loved.

Happiness

John had
Great Big
Waterproof
Boots on;
John had a
Great Big
Waterproof
Hat;
John had a
Great Big
Waterproof
Mackintosh—
And that
(Said John)
Is
That.

A. A. Milne

Toad by the Road

I'm only a toad
By the side of the road,
Watching the world go by.
Some hustle and hurry.
Some bustle and scurry.
Some wiggle, flicker, or fly.
They come and they go
On their way to and fro.
But I'd rather sit and sing.
It's a glorious day,
So I'm happy to stay
And savor the songs of spring.

Joanne Ryder

The Sun

I told the Sun that I was glad,
    I'm sure I don't know why;
Somehow the pleasant way he had
    Of shining in the sky
Just put a notion in my head
    That wouldn't it be fun
If, walking on the hill, I said
    "I'm happy" to the Sun.

John Drinkwater

How to Tell the Top of a Hill

The top of a hill
Is not until
The bottom is below.
And you have to stop
When you reach the top
For there's no more UP to go.

To make it plain
Let me explain:
The one *most* reason why
You have to stop
When you reach the top—is:
The next step up is sky.

John Ciardi

Afternoon on a Hill

I will be the gladdest thing
　　Under the sun!
I will touch a hundred flowers
　　And not pick one.

I will look at cliffs and clouds
　　With quiet eyes,
Watch the wind bow down the grass,
　　And the grass rise.

And when lights begin to show
　　Up from the town,
I will mark which must be mine,
　　And then start down!

Edna St. Vincent Millay

If-ing

If I had some small change
I'd buy me a mule,
Get on that mule and
Ride like a fool.

If I had some greenbacks
I'd buy me a Packard,
Fill it up with gas and
Drive that baby backward.

If I had a million
I'd get me a plane
And everybody in America'd
Think I was insane.

But I ain't got a million,
Fact is, ain't got a dime—
So just by *if*-ing
I have a good time!

Langston Hughes

Things

Went to the corner
Walked in the store
Bought me some candy
Ain't got it no more
Ain't got it no more

Went to the beach
Played on the shore
Built me a sandhouse
Ain't got it no more
Ain't got it no more

Went to the kitchen
Lay down on the floor
Made me a poem
Still got it
Still got it

Eloise Greenfield

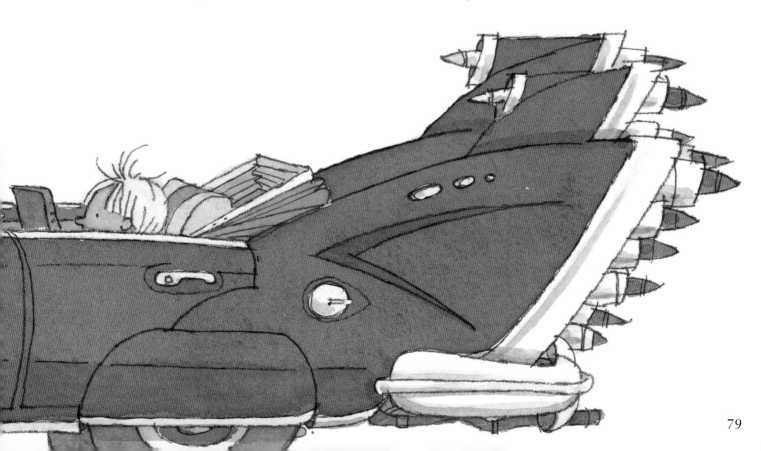

The Arrow and the Song

I shot an arrow into the air,
It fell to earth, I knew not where;
For, so swiftly it flew, the sight
Could not follow it in its flight.

I breathed a song into the air,
It fell to earth, I knew not where;
For who has sight so keen and strong,
That it can follow the flight of song?

Long, long afterward, in an oak
I found the arrow, still unbroke;
And the song, from beginning to end,
I found again in the heart of a friend.

Henry Wadsworth Longfellow

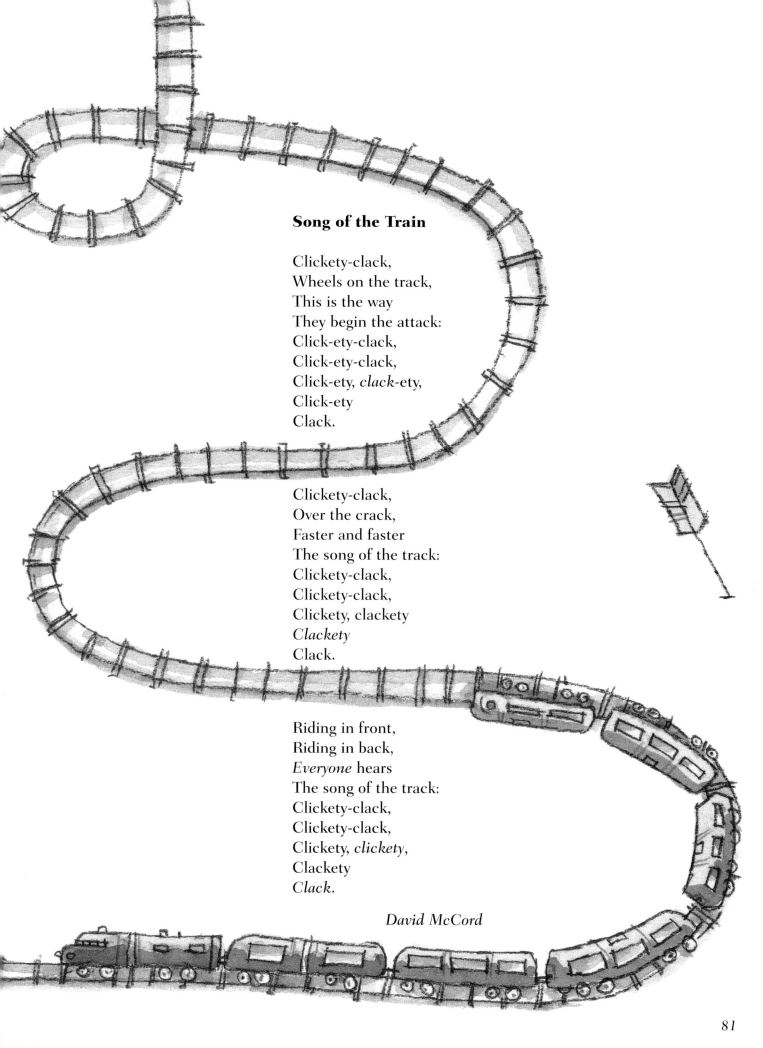

Song of the Train

Clickety-clack,
Wheels on the track,
This is the way
They begin the attack:
Click-ety-clack,
Click-ety-clack,
Click-ety, *clack*-ety,
Click-ety
Clack.

Clickety-clack,
Over the crack,
Faster and faster
The song of the track:
Clickety-clack,
Clickety-clack,
Clickety, clackety
Clackety
Clack.

Riding in front,
Riding in back,
Everyone hears
The song of the track:
Clickety-clack,
Clickety-clack,
Clickety, *clickety*,
Clackety
Clack.

David McCord

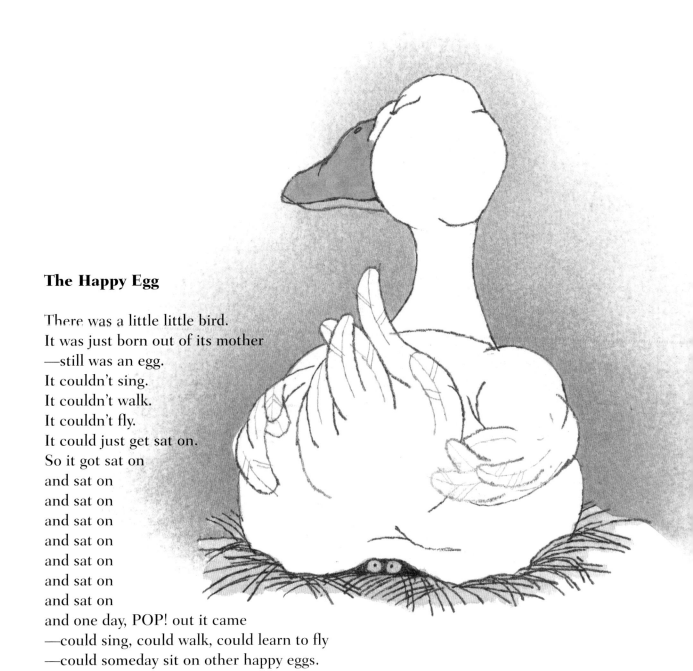

The Happy Egg

There was a little little bird.
It was just born out of its mother
—still was an egg.
It couldn't sing.
It couldn't walk.
It couldn't fly.
It could just get sat on.
So it got sat on
and sat on
and sat on
and sat on
and sat on
and sat on
and sat on
and sat on
and one day, POP! out it came
—could sing, could walk, could learn to fly
—could someday sit on other happy eggs.

Ruth Krauss

Jenny Kissed Me

Jenny kissed me when we met,
Jumping from the chair she sat in;
Time, you thief, who love to get
Sweets into your list, put that in!
Say I'm weary, say I'm sad,
Say that health and wealth have missed me,
Say I'm growing old, but add,
Jenny kissed me.

James Henry Leigh Hunt

There is a tree

There is a tree
that grows in me,
a tree
that no one else can see.
There is a bird
upon the tree,
upon the tree
that grows in me.
The tree that no one else can see.
And when the bird
upon the tree
begins to sing,
you think it's me.

Karla Kuskin

84

An Immorality

Sing we for love and idleness,
Naught else is worth the having.

Though I have been in many a land,
There is naught else in living.

And I would rather have my sweet,
Though rose-leaves die of grieving,

Than do high deeds in Hungary
To pass all men's believing.

Ezra Pound

WEATHER AND SEASONS

The season of the year and the weather of each day affect us in various ways. Bright sunny days usually cheer us up but sometimes can be too hot. Rainy days are often silvery and magical but at times may darken our mood. The first warm spring day after the cold of winter is greeted with joy, but the first snowfall is equally welcome.

Who Has Seen the Wind?

Who has seen the wind?
    Neither I nor you;
But when the leaves hang trembling
    The wind is passing through.

Who has seen the wind?
    Neither you nor I;
But when the trees bow down their heads
    The wind is passing by.

Christina Rossetti

Summer Grass

Summer grass aches and whispers.

It wants something; it calls and sings; it pours
   out wishes to the overhead stars.

The rain hears; the rain answers; the rain is slow
   coming; the rain wets the face of the grass.

Carl Sandburg

April Rain Song

Let the rain kiss you.
Let the rain beat upon your head with silver liquid drops.
Let the rain sing you a lullaby.

The rain makes still pools on the sidewalk.
The rain makes running pools in the gutter.
The rain plays a little sleep-song on our roof at night—

And I love the rain.

Langston Hughes

Over and Under

Bridges are for going over water,
Boats are for going over sea;
Dots are for going over dotted *i*'s,
And blankets are for going over me.

   Over and under,
    Over and under,
     Crack the whip,
      And hear the thunder.

Divers are for going under water,
Seals are for going under sea;
Fish are for going under mermaids' eyes,
And pillows are for going under me.

   Over and under,
    Over and under,
     Crack the whip,
      And hear the thunder,
       Crack-crack-crack,
        Hear the crack of thunder!

William Jay Smith

The Secret Song

Who saw the petals
    drop from the rose?
I, said the spider,
But nobody knows.

Who saw the sunset
    flash on a bird?
I, said the fish,
But nobody heard.

Who saw the fog
    come over the sea?
I, said the sea pigeon,
Only me.

Who saw the first
    green light of the sun?
I, said the night owl,
The only one.

Who saw the moss
    creep over the stone?
I, said the grey fox,
All alone.

Margaret Wise Brown

Fog

The fog comes
on little cat feet.

It sits looking
over harbor and city
on silent haunches
and then moves on.

Carl Sandburg

Snowspell

Look, it is falling a little
faster than falling, hurrying
straight down on urgent business
for snowbirds, snowballs, glaciers.

It is covering up the afternoon.
It is bringing the evening down
on top of us and soon the night.
It is falling fast as rain.

It is bringing shadows wide
as eagles' wings and dark
as crows over our heads.
It is falling, falling fast.

Robert Francis

Velvet Shoes

Let us walk in the white snow
    In a soundless space;
With footsteps quiet and slow,
    At a tranquil pace,
    Under veils of white lace.

I shall go shod in silk,
    And you in wool,
White as a white cow's milk,
    More beautiful
    Than the breast of a gull.

We shall walk through the still town
    In a windless peace;
We shall step upon white down,
    Upon silver fleece,
    Upon softer than these.

We shall walk in velvet shoes;
    Wherever we go
Silence will fall like dews
    On white silence below.
    We shall walk in the snow.

Elinor Wylie

Snow

Snow
Snow
Lots of snow
Everywhere we look and everywhere we go
Snow in the sandbox
Snow on the slide
Snow on the bicycle
Left outside
Snow on the steps
And snow on my feet
Snow on the sidewalk
Snow on the sidewalk
Snow on the sidewalk
Down the street.

Mary Ann Hoberman

I Heard a Bird Sing

I heard a bird sing
    In the dark of December
A magical thing
    And sweet to remember.

"We are nearer to Spring
    Than we were in September,"
I heard a bird sing
    In the dark of December.

Oliver Herford

SAD AND SORROWFUL

Everyone feels sad at one time or another. The causes
are many, from the death of a pet to a friend's moving
away to parents' divorce. The poems in this section
explore these and other reasons for sadness. They help
you to understand and empathize with the sorrows of
other creatures, both people and animals. They also
offer comfort and reassurance when you are unhappy.

Samuel

I found this salamander
Near a pond in the woods.
Samuel, I called him—
Samuel, Samuel.
Right away I loved him.
He loved me too, I think.
Samuel, I called him—
Samuel, Samuel.

I took him home in a coffee can,
And at night
He slept in my bed.
In the morning
I took him to school.

He died very quietly during spelling.

Sometimes I think
I should have left him
Near the pond in the woods.
Samuel, I called him—
Samuel, Samuel.

Bobbi Katz

Song

I had a dove, and the sweet dove died;
 And I have thought it died of grieving:
O, what could it grieve for? Its feet were tied
 With a silken thread of my own hand's weaving;
Sweet little red feet, why should you die—
Why should you leave me, sweet bird, why?
You lived alone in the forest tree,
Why, pretty thing! would you not live with me?
I kiss'd you oft and gave you white peas;
Why not live sweetly, as in the green trees?

John Keats

Poem

I loved my friend.
He went away from me.
There's nothing more to say.
The poem ends,
Soft as it began—
I loved my friend.

Langston Hughes

The Mouse

I heard a mouse
Bitterly complaining
In a crack of moonlight
Aslant on the floor—

"Little I ask
And that little is not granted.
There are few crumbs
In this world any more.

"The bread-box is tin
And I cannot get in.

"The jam's in a jar
My teeth cannot mar.

"The cheese sits by itself
On the pantry shelf—

"All night I run
Searching and seeking,
All night I run
About on the floor,

"Moonlight is there
And a bare place for dancing,
But no little feast
Is spread any more."

Elizabeth Coatsworth

The Flattered Flying Fish

Said the Shark to the Flying Fish over the phone:
"Will you join me tonight? I am dining alone.
Let me order a nice little dinner for two!
And come as you are, in your shimmering blue."

Said the Flying Fish: "Fancy remembering me,
And the dress that I wore at the Porpoises' tea!"
"How could I forget?" said the Shark in his guile:
"I expect you at eight!" and rang off with a smile.

She has powdered her nose; she has put on her things;
She is off with one flap of her luminous wings.
O little one, lovely, light-hearted and vain,
The Moon will not shine on your beauty again!

E. V. Rieu

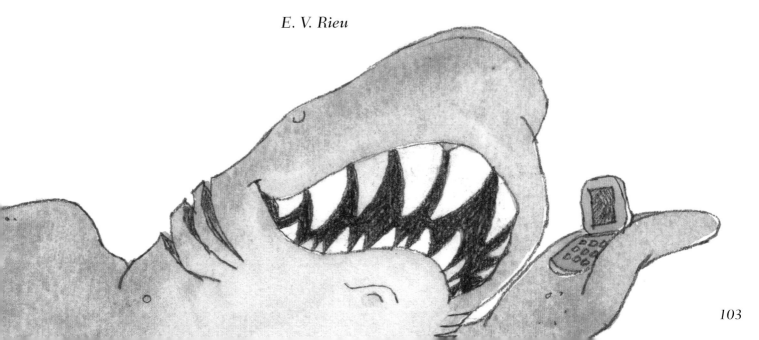

The Snare

I hear a sudden cry of pain!
    There is a rabbit in a snare;
Now I hear the cry again,
    But I cannot tell from where.

But I cannot tell from where.
    He is calling out for aid!
Crying on the frightened air,
    Making everything afraid!

Making everything afraid!
    Wrinkling up his little face!
As he cries again for aid;
    And I cannot find the place!

And I cannot find the place
    Where his paw is in the snare!
Little one! Oh, little one!
    I am searching everywhere!

James Stephens

My Father

My father doesn't live with us.
It doesn't help to make a fuss;
But still I feel unhappy, plus
   I miss him.

My father doesn't live with me.
He's got another family;
He moved away when I was three.
   I miss him.

I'm always happy on the day
He visits and we talk and play;
But after he has gone away
   I miss him.

Mary Ann Hoberman

Dust of Snow

The way a crow
Shook down on me
The dust of snow
From a hemlock tree

Has given my heart
A change of mood
And saved some part
Of a day I had rued.

Robert Frost

105

STRANGE AND MYSTERIOUS

There is something wonderfully strange about each of the poems in this section. It may be its sense; it may be its sound. It may be just a line or even a single word. Many of the poems take place at night, in darkness, with the moon shining and the wind howling. Whatever each poem's particular subject, at least a few of them will probably give you the shivers, especially once you learn them by heart.

The Horseman

I heard a horseman
    Ride over the hill;
The moon shone clear;
    The night was still;
His helmet was silver,
    And pale was he;
And the horse he rode
    Was of ivory.

Walter de la Mare

Windy Nights

Whenever the moon and stars are set,
　　Whenever the wind is high,
All night long in the dark and wet,
　　A man goes riding by.
Late in the night when the fires are out,
Why does he gallop and gallop about?

Whenever the trees are crying aloud,
　　And ships are tossed at sea,
By, on the highway, low and loud,
　　By at the gallop goes he.
By at the gallop he goes, and then
By he comes back at the gallop again.

　　　　　　Robert Louis Stevenson

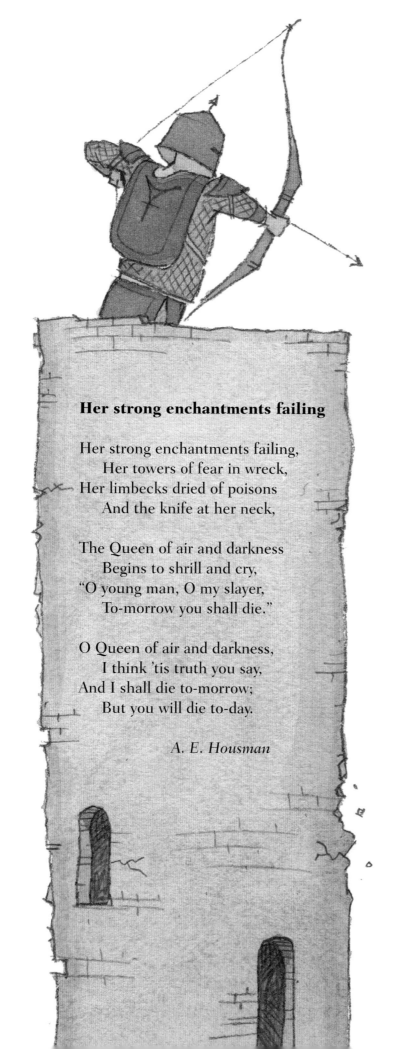

Her strong enchantments failing

Her strong enchantments failing,
    Her towers of fear in wreck,
Her limbecks dried of poisons
    And the knife at her neck,

The Queen of air and darkness
    Begins to shrill and cry,
"O young man, O my slayer,
    To-morrow you shall die."

O Queen of air and darkness,
    I think 'tis truth you say,
And I shall die to-morrow;
    But you will die to-day.

        A. E. Housman

Rapunzel

All day, all day I brush
    My golden strands of hair;
All day I wait and wait…
    Ah, who is there?

Who calls? Who calls? The gold
    Ladder of my long hair
I loose and wait…and wait…
    Ah, who is there?

She left at dawn…I am blind
    In the tangle of my long hair…
Is it she? the witch? the witch?
    Ah, who is there?

Adelaide Crapsey

Silver

Slowly, silently, now the moon
Walks the night in her silver shoon;
This way, and that, she peers, and sees
Silver fruit upon silver trees;
One by one the casements catch
Her beams beneath the silvery thatch;
Couched in his kennel, like a log,
With paws of silver sleeps the dog;
From their shadowy cote the white breasts peep
Of doves in a silver-feathered sleep;
A harvest mouse goes scampering by,
With silver claws, and silver eye;
And moveless fish in the water gleam,
By silver reeds in a silver stream.

Walter de la Mare

Where Go the Boats?

Dark brown is the river,
    Golden is the sand.
It flows along for ever,
    With trees on either hand.

Green leaves a-floating,
    Castles of the foam,
Boats of mine a-boating—
    Where will all come home?

On goes the river
    And out past the mill,
Away down the valley,
    Away down the hill.

Away down the river,
    A hundred miles or more,
Other little children
    Shall bring my boats ashore.

Robert Louis Stevenson

Dinky

O what's the weather in a Beard?
It's windy there, and rather weird,
And when you think the sky has cleared
    —Why, there is Dirty Dinky.

Suppose you walk out in a Storm,
With nothing on to keep you warm,
And then step barefoot on a Worm
    —Of course, it's Dirty Dinky.

As I was crossing a hot hot Plain,
I saw a sight that caused me pain,
You asked me before, I'll tell you again:
    —It *looked* like Dirty Dinky.

Last night you lay a-sleeping? No!
The room was thirty-five below;
The sheets and blankets turned to snow.
    —He'd got in: Dirty Dinky.

You'd better watch the things you do.
You'd better watch the things you do.
You're part of him; he's part of you
    —*You* may be Dirty Dinky.

Theodore Roethke

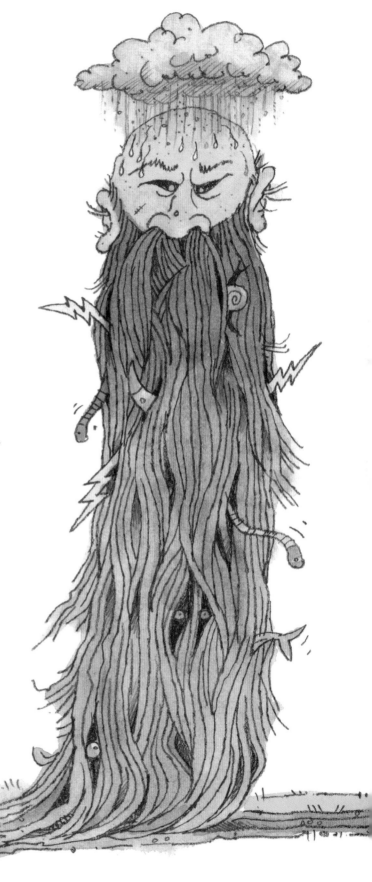

That Old Haunted House

That old haunted house was so creepy, so crawly, so
    ghastly, so ghostly, so gruesome, so skully-and-bony.
That old haunted house gave me nightmares and
    daymares and shudders and shivers and quivers and
    quavers and quakes.
That old haunted house made my hair stand on end and
    my heart pound-pound-pound and the blood in my
    veins ice-cold-freezing.
That old haunted house gave me goose bumps and
    throat lumps and ch-ch-ch-chattering teeth and the
    sh-sh-sh-shakes.
That old haunted house made me shriek, made me eeek,
    made me faint, made me scared-to-death scared,
    made me all-over sweat.
Would I ever go back to that old haunted house?
You bet.

Judith Viorst

The Mysterious Cat

I saw a proud, mysterious cat,
I saw a proud, mysterious cat
Too proud to catch a mouse or rat—
Mew, mew, mew.

But catnip she would eat, and purr,
But catnip she would eat, and purr.
And goldfish she did much prefer—
Mew, mew, mew.

I saw a cat—'twas but a dream,
I saw a cat—'twas but a dream
Who scorned the slave that brought her cream—
Mew, mew, mew.

Unless the slave were dressed in style,
Unless the slave were dressed in style
And knelt before her all the while—
Mew, mew, mew.

Did you ever hear of a thing like that?
Did you ever hear of a thing like that?
Did you ever hear of a thing like that?
Oh, what a proud mysterious cat.
Oh, what a proud mysterious cat.
Oh, what a proud mysterious cat.
Mew…mew…mew.

Vachel Lindsay

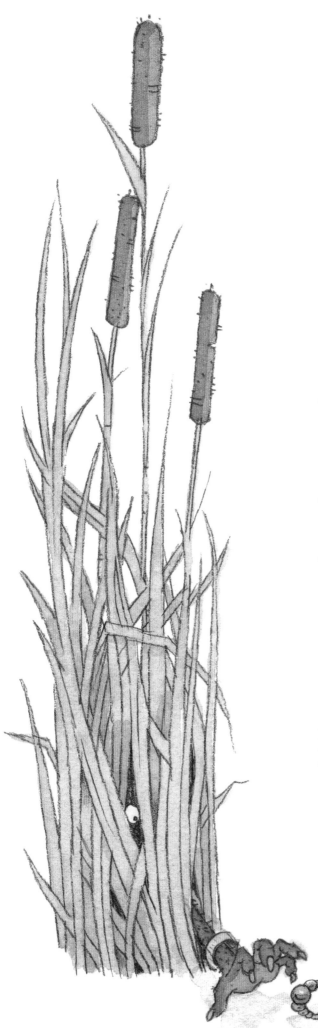

Overheard on a Saltmarsh

Nymph, nymph, what are your beads?

Green glass, goblin. Why do you stare at them?

Give them me.
                No.

Give them me. Give them me.

                        No.

Then I will howl all night in the reeds,
Lie in the mud and howl for them.

Goblin, why do you love them so?

They are better than stars or water,
Better than voices of winds that sing,
Better than any man's fair daughter,
Your green glass beads on a silver ring.

Hush, I stole them out of the moon.

Give me your beads. I want them.

                No.

I will howl in a deep lagoon
For your green glass beads, I love them so.
Give them me. Give them.

                No.

Harold Monro

Journey

So many towns not far from home,
So many towns where I might go,
So many people living there,
So many people I don't know.
Now what if in an unknown town,
An unknown town not far away,
An unknown person living there
Decides to take a walk one day?
And what if on that very day
I, too, decide to take a walk?
And what if on that very road
We meet halfway and start to talk
And tell each other secret things
As we go walking to and fro?
And what if we become good friends?
I'll start out now.
You never know.

Anne Marie Manfried

Old Man Ocean, how do you pound

Old Man Ocean, how do you pound
Smooth glass rough, rough stones round?
    Time and the tide and the wild waves rolling,
    Night and the wind and the long grey dawn.

Old Man Ocean, what do you tell,
What do you sing in the empty shell?
    Fog and the storm and the long bell tolling,
    Bones in the deep and the brave men gone.

        Russell Hoban

Ariel's Song

Full fathom five thy father lies;
    Of his bones are coral made;
Those are pearls that were his eyes;
Nothing of him that doth fade
But doth suffer a sea-change
Into something rich and strange.
Sea-nymphs hourly ring his knell:
                        Ding-dong.
Hark! Now I hear them—Ding-dong, bell.

William Shakespeare

POEMS FROM STORYBOOKS

Many writers of stories have written poetry as well.
Sometimes, as with the poems in this section, the
poems can be enjoyed whether or not you know the
stories they come from. Perhaps you will be tempted
to read some of the stories in order to find out where
the poems go and how they fit in. But first, enjoy the
poems on their own!

How Doth the Little Crocodile
(from *Alice in Wonderland*)

How doth the little crocodile
    Improve his shining tail,
And pour the waters of the Nile
    On every golden scale!

How cheerfully he seems to grin,
    How neatly spreads his claws,
And welcomes little fishes in,
    With gently smiling jaws!

Lewis Carroll

Ducks' Ditty
(from *The Wind in the Willows*)

All along the back water,
Through the rushes tall,
Ducks are a-dabbling,
Up tails all!

Ducks' tails, drakes' tails,
Yellow feet a-quiver,
Yellow bills all out of sight
Busy in the river!

Slushy green undergrowth
Where the roach swim—
Here we keep our larder,
Cool and full and dim.

Everyone for what he likes!
We like to be
Heads down, tails up,
Dabbling free!

High in the blue above
Swifts whirl and call—
We are down a-dabbling,
Up tails all!

Kenneth Grahame

**I am Rose my eyes are blue
(from *The World Is Round*)**

I am Rose my eyes are blue
I am Rose and who are you
I am Rose and when I sing
I am Rose like anything.

*Gertrude Stein
(abridged version)*

**I won't go down the horrible street
(from *The Wonderful O*)**

I won't go down the horrible street
To see the horrible people.
I'll gladly climb the terrible stair
That leads to the terrible steeple
And the terrible bats, and the terrible rats,
And the cats in the terrible steeple.
But I won't go down the horrible street
To see the horrible people.

James Thurber

Aunt Sponge and Aunt Spiker
(from *James and the Giant Peach*)

"I look and smell," Aunt Sponge declared, "as lovely
    as a rose!
Just feast your eyes upon my face, observe my
    shapely nose!
Behold my heavenly silky locks!
And if I take off both my socks
You'll see my dainty toes."
"But don't forget," Aunt Spiker cried, "how much your
    tummy shows!"

Aunt Sponge went red. Aunt Spiker said, "My sweet,
    you cannot win,
Behold MY gorgeous curvy shape, my teeth,
    my charming grin!
Oh, beauteous me! How I adore
My radiant looks! And please ignore
The pimple on my chin."
"My dear old trout!" Aunt Sponge cried out, "You're only
    bones and skin!"

"Such loveliness as I possess can only truly shine
In Hollywood!" Aunt Sponge declared. "Oh, wouldn't
    that be fine!
I'd capture all the nations' hearts!
They'd give me all the leading parts!
The stars would all resign!"
"I think you'd make," Aunt Spiker said, "a lovely
    Frankenstein."

Roald Dahl

In and out the bushes, up the ivy
(from *The Bat-Poet*)

In and out the bushes, up the ivy,
Into the hole
By the old oak stump, the chipmunk flashes.
Up the pole

To the feeder full of seeds he dashes,
Stuffs his cheeks,
The chickadee and titmouse scold him.
Down he streaks.

Red as the leaves the wind blows off the maple,
Red as a fox,
Striped like a skunk, the chipmunk whistles
Past the love seat, past the mailbox,

Down the path,
Home to his warm hole stuffed with sweet
Things to eat.
Neat and slight and shining, his front feet

Curled at his breast, he sits there while the sun
Stripes the red west
With its last light: the chipmunk
Dives to his rest.

Randall Jarrell

**The Road goes ever on and on
(from *The Fellowship of the Ring*)**

The Road goes ever on and on
    Down from the door where it began.
Now far ahead the Road has gone,
    And I must follow, if I can,
Pursuing it with eager feet,
    Until it joins some larger way
Where many paths and errands meet.
    And whither then? I cannot say.

J. R. R. Tolkien

THE LONG OF IT

In this section you are offered a challenge. These are long poems, by far the longest in the book. Now that you have learned many shorter poems by heart, perhaps you might want to attempt one of these. You may find that they are not much harder than some of the poems you have mastered. They all rhyme, they all have regular strong rhythm and lots of repetition, and they all are funny. Give them a try!

The Jumblies

I They went to sea in a Sieve, they did,
     In a Sieve they went to sea:
In spite of all their friends could say,
On a winter's morn, on a stormy day,
     In a Sieve they went to sea!
And when the Sieve turned round and round,
And every one cried, "You'll all be drowned!"
They called aloud, "Our Sieve ain't big,
But we don't care a button! we don't care a fig!
     In a Sieve we'll go to sea!"
       Far and few, far and few,
         Are the lands where the Jumblies live;
       Their heads are green, and their hands are blue,
         And they went to sea in a Sieve.

II They sailed away in a Sieve, they did,
     In a Sieve they sailed so fast,
With only a beautiful pea-green veil
Tied with a riband by way of a sail,
     To a small tobacco-pipe mast;
And everyone said, who saw them go,
"O won't they soon be upset, you know!
For the sky is dark, and the voyage is long,
And happen what may, it's extremely wrong
     In a Sieve to sail so fast."
       Far and few, far and few,
         Are the lands where the Jumblies live;
       Their heads are green, and their hands are blue,
         And they went to sea in a Sieve.

III The water it soon came in, it did,
     The water it soon came in;
So to keep them dry, they wrapped their feet
In a pinky paper all folded neat,
     And they fastened it down with a pin.
And they passed the night in a crockery-jar,
And each of them said, "How wise we are!
Though the sky be dark, and the voyage be long,
Yet we never can think we were rash or wrong,
     While round in our Sieve we spin!"
       Far and few, far and few,
         Are the lands where the Jumblies live;
       Their heads are green, and their hands are blue,
         And they went to sea in a Sieve.

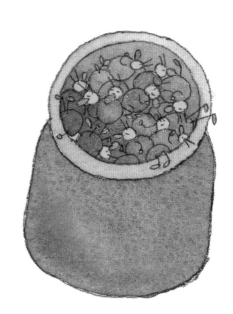

IV And all night long they sailed away;
       And when the sun went down,
   They whistled and warbled a moony song
   To the echoing sound of a coppery gong,
       In the shade of the mountains brown.
   "O Timballo! How happy we are,
   When we live in a sieve and a crockery-jar,
   And all night long in the moonlight pale,
   We sail away with a pea-green sail,
   In the shade of the mountains brown!"
       Far and few, far and few,
           Are the lands where the Jumblies live;
       Their heads are green, and their hands are blue,
           And they went to sea in a Sieve.

V They sailed to the Western Sea, they did,
       To a land all covered with trees,
   And they bought an Owl, and a useful Cart,
   And a pound of Rice, and a Cranberry Tart,
       And a hive of silvery Bees.
   And they bought a Pig, and some green Jack-daws,
   And a lovely Monkey with lollipop paws,
   And forty bottles of Ring-Bo-Ree,
       And no end of Stilton Cheese.
           Far and few, far and few,
               Are the lands where the Jumblies live;
           Their heads are green, and their hands are blue,
               And they went to sea in a Sieve.

VI And in twenty years they all came back,
       In twenty years or more,
   And every one said, "How tall they've grown!
   For they've been to the Lakes, and the Torrible Zone,
       And the hills of the Chankly Bore";
   And they drank their health, and gave them a feast
   Of dumplings made of beautiful yeast;
   And every one said, "If we only live
   We too will go to sea in a Sieve
       To the hills of the Chankly Bore!"
           Far and few, far and few,
               Are the lands where the Jumblies live;
           Their heads are green, and their hands are blue,
               And they went to sea in a Sieve.

Edward Lear

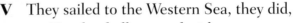

131

Disobedience

James James
Morrison Morrison
Weatherby George Dupree
Took great
Care of his Mother,
Though he was only three.
James James
Said to his Mother,
"Mother," he said, said he;
"You must never go down to the end of the town, if you
don't go down with me."

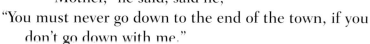

James James
Morrison's Mother
Put on a golden gown,
James James
Morrison's Mother
Drove to the end of the town.
James James
Morrison's Mother
Said to herself, said she:
"I can get right down to the end of the town and be back in
time for tea."

King John
Put up a notice,
"LOST or STOLEN or STRAYED!
JAMES JAMES
MORRISON'S MOTHER
SEEMS TO HAVE BEEN MISLAID.
LAST SEEN
WANDERING VAGUELY:
QUITE OF HER OWN ACCORD,
SHE TRIED TO GET DOWN TO THE END OF THE
TOWN—FORTY SHILLINGS REWARD!"

James James
Morrison Morrison
(Commonly known as Jim)
Told his
Other relations
Not to go blaming *him*.
James James
Said to his Mother,
"Mother," he said, said he;
"You must *never* go down to the end of the town without
   consulting me."

James James
Morrison's mother
Hasn't been heard of since.
King John
Said he was sorry,
So did the Queen and Prince
King John
(Somebody told me)
Said to a man he knew:
"If people go down to the end of the town, well, what can
   anyone do?"

(Now then, very softly)

J. J.
M. M.
W. G. Du P.
Took great
C/o his M*****
Though he was only 3.
J. J.
Said to his M*****
"M*****," he said, said he:
"You-must-never-go-down-to-the-end-of-the-town-if-you-
   don't-go-down-with ME!"

A. A. Milne

The Camel's Hump

The Camel's hump is an ugly lump
    Which well you may see at the Zoo;
But uglier yet is the hump we get
    From having too little to do.

Kiddies and grown-ups too-oo-oo,
If we haven't enough to do-oo-oo,
    We get the hump—
    Cameelious hump—
The hump that is black and blue!

We climb out of bed with a frouzly head
    And a snarly-yarly voice.
We shiver and scowl and we grunt and we growl
    At our bath and our boots and our toys;

And there ought to be a corner for me
(And I know there is one for you)
    When we get the hump—
    Cameelious hump—
The hump that is black and blue!

The cure for this ill is not to sit still,
    Or frowst with a book by the fire;
But to take a large hoe and a shovel also,
    And dig till you gently perspire;

And then you will find that the sun and the wind,
And the Djinn of the Garden too,
    Have lifted the hump—
    The horrible hump—
The hump that is black and blue!

I get it as well as you-oo-oo—
If I haven't enough to do-oo-oo—
    We all get hump—
    Cameelious hump—
Kiddies and grown-ups too!

Rudyard Kipling

The Camel's Complaint

Canary-birds feed on sugar and seed,
    Parrots have crackers to crunch;
And as for the poodles, they tell me the noodles
    Have chicken and cream for their lunch.
      But there's never a question
      About *my* digestion—
        Anything does for me.

Cats, you're aware, can repose in a chair,
    Chickens can roost upon rails;
Puppies are able to sleep in a stable,
    And oysters can slumber in pails.
      But no one supposes
      A poor camel dozes—
        Any place does for me.

Lambs are enclosed where it's never exposed,
    Coops are constructed for hens;
Kittens are treated to houses well heated,
    And pigs are protected by pens.
      But a camel comes handy
      Wherever it's sandy—
        Anywhere does for me.

People would laugh if you rode a giraffe,
    Or mounted the back of an ox;
It's nobody's habit to ride on a rabbit,
    Or try to bestraddle a fox.
      But as for the camel, he's
      Ridden by families—
        Any load does for me.

A snake is as round as a hole in the ground,
    And weasels are wavy and sleek;
And no alligator could ever be straighter
    Than lizards that live in a creek.
      But a camel's all lumpy
      And bumpy and humpy—
        Any shape does for me.

Charles E. Carryl

The Llama Who Had No Pajama

The llama who had no pajama
Was troubled and terribly sad
When it became known that he had outgrown
Every pair of pajamas he had;
And he tearfully said to his mama
In a voice that was deep with despair:
O llamaly mama
I need a pajama
Or what in the world will I wear?
Or what in the world,
In the wumberly world,
In the wumberly world will I wear?

The llama who had no pajama
Looked up at the evening sky.
It will soon, he said, be time for bed
And all will be sleeping but I.
And all will be sleeping but I, but I,
And all will be sleeping but I.
For how can a llama go bare to bed,
The little pajamaless llama said,
When the rest of the world,
Of the wumberly world,
Are all wearing pretty pajamas?

The poor little llama's sad mama
Got out her needle and thread.
I'll try to enlarge your pajama,
The llama's sad mama said.
And she stitched and she sewed those pajamas
Till she ran out of plum-colored thread,
But they still were too small for the llama.
O what will we do? Mama said.
For you must have a pair of pajamas
As you cannot go naked to bed;
But where in the world,
In the wumberly world,
Will we find you a pair of pajamas?

They looked in each nook and each cranny;
They looked on each hillock and mound;
But though they saw bathrobes and bonnets,
Pajamas were not to be found.
The clock struck a quarter to seven.
The llama lay down on the ground.
I know I won't sleep, he sniffed sadly,
And his nose made a staying-up sound.

But he did sleep. He dozed off at seven,
And he slept for the rest of the night;
And when he woke up in the morning
To his mama he said with delight:
What a wonderful sleep I've been sleeping all night!
My head feels so clear and my eyes feel so bright.
When we looked for pajamas, how foolish we were.
Why, I sleep so much better in nothing but fur!
It fits me so nicely; it's light as the air;
It's the practical thing for a llama to wear.
And since goats don't wear coats
And doves don't wear gloves
And cocks don't wear socks
And bats don't wear hats,
Well, why in the world,
In the wumberly world,
Should llamas be wearing pajamas?

Mary Ann Hoberman

SOME SUGGESTIONS FOR LEARNING POETRY BY HEART

The first thing to do with any poem you want to learn by heart is to read it aloud several times. Read it slowly, for the sense, giving each word its natural weight and rhythm. Notice where the accents fall in each line, whether a phrase ends at a line break or continues into the next line. If the poem rhymes, notice the rhyming scheme and take that into consideration. If it doesn't, see whether there might be rhyming words within the lines that call out to you.

Begin with one of the shorter poems, one with regular rhyme and rhythm. Limericks, with their bouncy five-line format, are especially catchy and easy to commit to memory.

But these brief verses are also training wheels for longer, more complex poems. The many forms of repetition within any given poem, of sounds and words and sometimes entire phrases, knit the poem together, just as in a painting the various repeated colors and shapes tie the parts into the whole. These repetitions please your ear and probably set off vibrations in your body as well. They are also the building blocks you use to reconstruct the poem inside yourself.

I like to think of the process of learning a poem by heart as a game, with the memorized poem as the prize. As in any game, there are rules to follow, and you improve with practice. Let's start with the first couplet of "Old Man Ocean, how do you pound" (Russell Hoban, p. 118):

> Old Man Ocean, how do you pound
> Smooth glass rough, rough stones round?

First of all, what do you see in your mind's eye? Here, the ocean is personified as a huge old man composed of great swells of water, pounding away at the objects caught in its waves. You hear the heavy drumbeat of the accented syllables—you might even clap them out—mimicking the ocean's pounding:

> <u>Old</u> Man <u>O</u>cean, <u>how</u> do you <u>pound</u>
> Smooth glass <u>rough</u>, <u>rough</u> stones <u>round</u>?

While sound is always primary, the poet is also concerned with how the poem looks on the page. Notice the visual clues the two lines offer: the word repetitions and resemblances; the preponderance of *o*'s, with their various pronunciations; the fact that *ou* sounds different in *you* and *rough* and *round*. Hear how *smooth*, with its double *o*'s, really does sound *smoooth* and wants to be pronounced that way.

Move on to the next couplet:

> *Time and the tide and the wild waves rolling,*
> *Night and the wind and the long grey dawn.*

Look and listen. The *i* has replaced the *o* almost entirely. Clap out the lines again. Notice that while the strong accents are similar to those in the first couplet, each line has been given two extra weak syllables, all four the same word: *the*. And there are more repetitions of word beginnings (alliteration) and interiors (assonance), all pleasing to the ear and helpful to the memory.

The more you look at and listen to the lines, the more you see and hear in them. And the more you see and hear in them, the better you remember them. Couplet by couplet you continue, repeating the words aloud and listening to how they sound, visualizing the pictures they call up in your mind, exploring different ways of speaking them, louder and softer, more or less accented. Each time you learn a couplet by heart, you add it to the previous ones you've already memorized, and before you know it, you have the entire poem.

Now the real fun begins! Saying the entire poem to yourself again and again, you start to *feel* why the poet chose particular sounds and cadences. With each repetition of the poem, new insights occur to you. Eventually the poem becomes so much a part of you that you can almost believe you made it up yourself. It is at this moment that you truly own the poem.

And you will have it for the rest of your life!

INDEX OF FIRST LINES

Francisco X. Alarcón: "San Francisco" from *Iguanas in the Snow and Other Winter Poems/Iguanas en la nieve y otros poemas de invierno*, copyright © 2001 by Francisco X. Alarcón, reprinted by permission of Children's Book Press, San Francisco, www.childrensbookpress.org.

Rosemary and Stephen Vincent Benét: "Nancy Hanks" by Rosemary Carr Benét from *A Book of Americans* by Rosemary and Stephen Vincent Benét (Henry Holt & Company), copyright © 1933 by Rosemary and Stephen Vincent Benét, renewed copyright © 1961 by Rosemary Carr Benét, reprinted by permission of Brandt & Hochman Literary Agents, Inc.

Gwendolyn Brooks: "Marie Lucille," reprinted by consent of Brooks Permissions.

Margaret Wise Brown: "The Secret Song," copyright © 1959 by William R. Scott, Inc., renewed 1987 by Roberta Rauch, used by permission of HarperCollins Publishers.

Carl Carmer: "Antique Shop" from *French Town* by Carl Carmer, copyright © 1968, used by permission of the licenser, Pelican Publishing Company, Inc.

John Ciardi: "How to Tell the Top of a Hill" from *The Reason for the Pelican*, reprinted by permission of the author.

Elizabeth Coatsworth: "Pretty Futility" and "The Mouse" from *Compass Rose* by Elizabeth Coatsworth, copyright © 1929 by Coward-McCann, Inc., renewed © 1957 by Elizabeth Coatsworth, used by permission of Coward-McCann, Inc., a division of Penguin Young Readers Group, a member of Penguin Group (USA), Inc., 345 Hudson Street, New York, NY 10014, all rights reserved; "Roosters," reprinted by permission of Paterson Marsh Ltd. on behalf of the Estate of Elizabeth Coatsworth.

Roald Dahl: "Aunt Sponge and Aunt Spiker" from *James and the Giant Peach* by Roald Dahl, copyright © 1961, renewed 1989 by Roald Dahl, used by permission of Alfred A. Knopf, an imprint of Random House Children's Books, a division of Random House, Inc.

Emily Dickinson: "A word is dead" from *The Poems of Emily Dickinson*, Thomas H. Johnson, ed., Cambridge, Mass.: The Belknap Press of Harvard University Press, copyright © 1951, 1955, 1979, 1983 by the president and fellows of Harvard College, reprinted by permission of the publishers and the Trustees of Amherst College.

Barbara Esbensen: "My Cat," copyright © 1992 by Barbara Juster Esbensen, used by permission of HarperCollins Publishers.

Rachel Field: "The Animal Store" from *Taxis and Toadstools* by Rachel Field, copyright © 1926 by Doubleday, a division of Random House, Inc., used by permission of Doubleday, an imprint of Random House Children's Books, a division of Random House, Inc.

Aileen Fisher: "Bird Talk," used by permission of Marian Reiner on behalf of the Boulder Public Library Foundation, Inc.

Douglas Florian: "The Puffin" from *zoo's who*, copyright © 2005 by Douglas Florian, reprinted by permission of Houghton Mifflin Harcourt Publishing Company.

Robert Francis: "Snowspell" from *Like Ghosts of Eagles*, reprinted with the permission of the University of Massachusetts Press.

Robert Frost: "A Time to Talk" and "Dust of Snow" from *The Poetry of Robert Frost*, edited by Edward Connery Lathem, copyright © 1916, 1923, 1969 by Henry Holt and Company, copyright © 1944, 1951 by Robert Frost, reprinted by permission of Henry Holt and Company, LLC.

Rose Fyleman: "Mary Middling," reprinted by permission of the Society of Authors as the Literary Representative of the Estate of Rose Fyleman.

Kristine O'Connell George: "At Night" from *Old Elm Speaks: Tree Poems* by Kristine O'Connell George, text copyright © 1998 by Kristine O'Connell George, reprinted by permission of Clarion Books, an imprint of Houghton Mifflin Harcourt Publishing Company, all rights reserved.

Nikki Giovanni: "poem for rodney" from *Spin a Soft Black Song* (revised edition) by Nikki Giovanni, illustrated by George Martins, copyright © 1971, 1985 by Nikki Giovanni, reprinted by permission of Hill and Wang, a division of Farrar, Straus and Giroux, LLC.

Eloise Greenfield: "Things," text copyright © 1978 by Eloise Greenfield, used by permission of HarperCollins Publishers.

Nikki Grimes: "You Oughta Meet Danitra Brown," text copyright © 1994 by Nikki Grimes, used by permission of HarperCollins Publishers.

Georgia Heard: "Bat Patrol" from *Creatures of Earth, Sea, and Sky* by Georgia Heard (Boyds Mills Press), copyright © 1997 by Georgia Heard, reprinted by permission.

Russell Hoban: "Old Man Ocean, how do you pound" from *The Pedaling Man and Other Poems*, copyright © 1968 by Russell Hoban, reprinted by permission of Harold Ober Associates Incorporated.

Mary Ann Hoberman: "Auk Talk" from *The Llama Who Had No Pajama: 100 Favorite Poems*, copyright © 1973 by Mary Ann Hoberman, reproduced by permission of Houghton Mifflin Harcourt Publishing Company; "Fireflies" from *The Llama Who Had No Pajama: 100 Favorite Poems*, copyright © 1976 by Mary Ann Hoberman, reproduced by permission of Houghton Mifflin Harcourt Publishing Company; "Hippopotamus" and "Yellow Butter" from *The Llama Who Had No Pajama: 100 Favorite Poems*, copyright © 1981 by Mary Ann Hoberman, reproduced by permission of Houghton Mifflin Harcourt Publishing Company; "My Father" from *Fathers, Mothers, Sisters, Brothers: A Collection of Family Poems* by Mary Ann Hoberman, illustrated by Marylin Hafner, copyright © 1991 by Mary Ann Hoberman, reprinted by permission of Little, Brown and Company; "Oak Leaf Plate" from *The Llama Who Had No Pajama: 100 Favorite Poems*, copyright © 1965 by Mary Ann Hoberman, reproduced by permission of Houghton Mifflin Harcourt Publishing Company; "Sometimes" from *Fathers, Mothers, Sisters, Brothers: A Collection of Family Poems* by Mary Ann Hoberman, illustrated by Marylin Hafner, copyright © 1991 by Mary Ann Hoberman, reprinted by permission of Little, Brown and Company. "Time," "Tiger," "How Far," "Snow," and "The Llama Who Had No Pajama" (which originally appeared in *Hello and Good-by*) from *The Llama Who Had No Pajama: 100 Favorite Poems*, copyright © 1959 by Mary Ann Hoberman, reproduced by permission of Houghton Mifflin Harcourt Publishing Company.

Lee Bennett Hopkins: "My Name," copyright © 1974 by Lee Bennett Hopkins, reprinted by permission of Curtis Brown, Ltd.

Patricia Hubbell: "The Oak Trees Are Dreaming" from *Black Earth, Gold Sun* by Patricia Hubbell, copyright © 2001 by Patricia Hubbell, used by permission of Marian Reiner for the author.

Langston Hughes: "April Rain Song," "If-ing," and "Poem" from *The Collected Poems of Langston Hughes* by Langston Hughes, edited by Arnold Rampersad with David Roessel, associate editor, copyright © 1994 by the Estate of Langston Hughes, used by permission of Alfred A. Knopf, a division of Random House, Inc.

Randall Jarrell: "In and out the bushes, up the ivy," copyright © 1964 by the Macmillan Company, copyright © renewed 1992 by Mary Jarrell, used by permission of HarperCollins Publishers.

Bobbi Katz: "Samuel," copyright © 1972 by Bobbi Katz, who controls all rights.

Ruth Krauss: "The Happy Egg," copyright © 2005 by the Estate of Ruth Krauss, used by permission of HarperCollins Publishers.

To my beloved Norman
—M.A.H.

For Norm and Mary Ann, whose strength and determination during the making
of this book made it unthinkable to give anything less than my very best
—M.E.

The illustrations for this book were done in pencil, watercolor, and pastel on
185 gsm Arches watercolor papers.
The text and the display type are set in Fairfield.
Book design by Saho Fujii

Little, Brown and Company

Hachette Book Group
237 Park Avenue, New York, NY 10017
Visit our website at www.lb-kids.com

Little, Brown and Company is a division of Hachette Book Group, Inc.
The Little, Brown name and logo are trademarks of Hachette Book Group, Inc.

The publisher is not responsible for websites (or their content) that are not owned by the publisher.

First Edition: April 2012

Library of Congress Cataloging-in-Publication Data
Forget-me-nots : poems to learn by heart / compiled by Mary Ann Hoberman ; illustrated by Michael Emberley.—1st ed.
p. cm.
ISBN 978-0-316-12947-3
1. Children's poetry, American. I. Hoberman, Mary Ann. II. Emberley, Michael.
PS586.3.F67 2012
811.008'09282—dc23
2011025119

10 9 8 7 6 5 4 3 2 1

SC

Printed in China